LILY
THE UNICORN

BY DALLAS CLAYTON

HARPER

An Imprint of HarperCollinsPublishers

ISBN 978-0-06-211668-0 (trade bdg.)

The artist used magic crystals and wild abandon to create the illustrations for this book.
Book design by Victor Joseph Ochoa
17   SCP   10 9 8 7 6 5
❖
First Edition

To anyone who's
ever felt different.

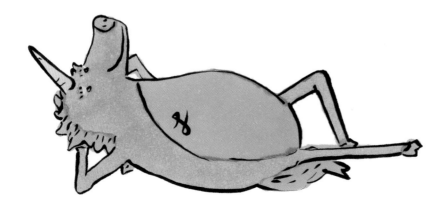

I LIKE MAKING MUSIC.

SAXOPHONE

DRUMS

PIANO

TRUMPET

CELLO

BANJO

ACCORDION

SINGING

XYLOPHONE

FLUTE

ALLIGATOR BILL

JASPER

WILFREDO

CANNONBALL THE CRAB

CORTEZ THE CAT

JEREMY JOE

RJ THE RAT

TODAY I MADE A NEW FRIEND.

HIS NAME IS ROGER!

HIS FAVORITE COLOR IS GRAY.

HIS FAVORITE PLACE IS INSIDE.

HIS FAVORITE HOBBY IS ORGANIZING BLANK PAPER.

HIS FAVORITE DANCE IS SITTING DOWN.

HIS FAVORITE BOOK IS EMPTY.

HIS FAVORITE SMELL IS PLAIN.

HIS FAVORITE FOOD IS WARM WATER.

HIS FAVORITE ANIMAL IS HIMSELF.

HIS FAVORITE SONG IS QUIET.

HIS FAVORITE TIME OF DAY IS "NOT RIGHT NOW."

HIS FAVORITE SPORT IS RESTING.

HIS FAVORITE DESTINATION IS NOWHERE.

HIS FAVORITE STORE IS CLOSED.

HIS FAVORITE TOY IS A BRIEFCASE.

SO I PLANNED SOME ADVENTURES FOR US TO SEEK OUT,

SAILING THE SEAS

ON THE BACKS OF ELEPHANTS

UNDERWATER

THROUGH THE DARKEST JUNGLES

DEEP INTO THE EARTH

DOMINOES

BASKETBALL

DODGEBALL

FREEZE TAG

TIC-TAC-TOE

BUT
HE
WAS
NOT
IMPRESSED.

GOLF

"WE COULD INVENT NEW PLANETS!"
ZOONDOPIA
WATER PLANET
MARS #2
POWER SUN
FANTASTICALASOTY
DOG PLANET
BLAMO!

"WE COULD BUILD A HELICOPTER, PRETEND WE ARE BUTTERFLIES, HYPNOTIZE EACH OTHER,

TAME A WILD DRAGON, FIND ALL THE SECRETS, TELL THE BEST STORIES, DANCE AND ♫ DANCE AND DANCE AND DANCE..."

AND THERE'S JUST SO MUCH

 RIDE A UNICYCLE

 SCULPT A VASE

 MAKE A PIE

 TELL A JOKE

 MILK A COW

FIND A DIAMOND

 FOLD ORIGAMI

SURF A WAVE

 DO KARATE

VACUUM A STADIUM

PROGRAM A COMPUTER

 RAISE A KITTEN

KICK A FIELD GOAL

 SOUND A HORN

 GROW A TOMATO

 HIT A BULL'S-EYE

 CRACK A PIÑATA

AND WHAT HAPPENS IF I TRY AND I FAIL? YOU'RE TELLING ME I CAN GET RIGHT BACK UP AND KEEP ON SMILING? TRAVELING AROUND AND EXPLORING

AND MAKING FRIENDS? YOU'RE TELLING ME THERE'S ALL KINDS OF FUN JUST WAITING FOR ME?!?